SAVING HANNO

SAVING HANNO

Miriam Halahmy

HOLIDAY HOUSE NEW YORK

HOLIDAY HOUSE is registered in the U.S. Patent and Trademark Office.
Printed and bound in October 2022 at Maple Press, York, PA, USA.
www.holidayhouse.com

First hardcover edition published in 2019
First paperback edition published in 2022
 5 7 9 10 8 6 4

Library of Çongress Cataloging-in-Publication Data

Names: Halahmy, Miriam, author.
Title: Saving Hanno / Miriam Halahmy.
Description: First edition. | New York : Holiday House, [2019] | Summary:
    Nine-year-old Rudi and his beloved dachshund, Hanno, face peril as they
    are being sent from Nazi Germany to England on special trains called
    Kindertransports during World War II. Includes historical note.
Identifiers: LCCN 2018023303 | ISBN 9780823441655 (hardcover)
Subjects: | CYAC: Refugees—Fiction. | Dachshunds—Fiction. | Dogs—Fiction.
    Kindertransports (rescue operations)—Fiction. | Jews—Germany—
    History—1933–1945—Fiction. | World War, 1939–1945—Refugees—Fiction.
Classification: LCC PZ7.H12825 Sav 2019 | DDC [Fic]—dc23
LC record available at https://lccn.loc.gov/2018023303

ISBN: 978-0-8234-4165-5 (hardcover)
ISBN: 978-0-8234-4670-4 (paperback)
ISBN: 978-0-8234-4218-8 (eBook)

For Samuel
with love

Contents

1. A New Teacher

Monday, November 21, 1938

"I wish school would burn down. Don't you, Rudi?" says Emil, my best friend, his leather bag bumping on his back. "Why didn't that mob set fire to it when they burned the synagogue?"

It's more than a week since anyone went to school. This has been so boring for a boy like me.

Eleven days ago, Nazi gangs ran down our street and all over town, smashing windows and setting fires and other bad stuff. It was very scary even though I wasn't allowed to look through the curtains and see anything.

Mutti wouldn't let me go out for days. My older sister, Lotte, was allowed out a bit, of course; she's fifteen. No one told me anything about what had happened.

They just kept saying, "Don't worry, Rudi, it's all fine."

But Mutti has two deep lines across her forehead now, and she looks nervous all the time. She watches the clock all day when Papa's out at work.

Papa is a newspaper journalist and Mutti told him, "Be careful what you write; don't give them any reason."

When I asked, "Any reason for what?" no one answered me.

It's not fair.

❧

It's been horrible being stuck at home for so long.

We have a second-floor apartment with three bedrooms and a big living room facing the street. Papa has a little study next to the bathroom, and the kitchen looks out over the back and more apartment buildings. My bedroom faces the street too and I like playing with my toys in there. But when you're indoors all the time, you feel sort of squashed up and everyone gets bad-tempered.

At least I had Hanno to play with. He's my little dachshund, and he's the best dog in the whole wide world. I've had him since he was a puppy. He's two years and one month old now. He goes everywhere with me, except school, of course.

Hanno's coat is very smooth and a sort of chocolate brown. His ears feel like the velvet on Mutti's best dress. His legs are quite short, but he can walk and run long distances—all the way to the park and even as far as Emil's apartment, which is near the main square.

Hanno is very clever. I've been training him to do tricks. He can almost count to three now, I think. His best trick is collecting the letters. He sits on the mat at the front door and as soon as a letter drops through, he picks it up in his mouth and carries it to me. He hardly ever gets it wet or chews up the corners.

When I stare into Hanno's brown eyes he stares back without blinking, and I'm pretty sure he can read my mind. Emil and I tried an experiment once.

I thought and thought about cinnamon cookies—Hanno's favorite, Mutti makes a ton every week—and Hanno ran into the kitchen and pointed his long brown nose up toward the cookie tin, barking like a lunatic.

"See?" I said to Emil.

"Amazing," said Emil, with his wide grin.

~

"If school burned down, what would we do all day?" I say now as we walk on the road that runs by the river.

Our city's called Frankfurt am Main because it's on the River Main. It's quite a lot to spell out. I could do it by the time I was five, but Emil still can't even spell *Frankfurt* and we're nearly nine now. That's why Emil hates school.

"'S'easy," he declares. "We'd play all day in the park with Hanno. Race you!"

Emil's taller than me and he can run like the wind. I follow, my schoolbag bumping on my back, and arrive puffing behind him at the school gates.

But then my stomach does a flip. Konrad Müller is there with his gang. They're much bigger than us, and they're all

Hitler Youth. Jews can't join the Hitler Youth, which is a bit unfair because they have a uniform and go camping and everything. They bully Emil and me and the other Jewish kids.

"Germany has changed," Papa says every day, tapping the newspaper, his hand running back through his dark, wavy hair. "Hitler's made this country stink."

"Then let's go to Palestine!" cries out Lotte, her brown eyes flashing.

We all have brown eyes and olive skin that tans deep brown in summer. My dark brown hair is wavy like Papa's, but Lotte and Mutti have straight brown hair. We're all quite short, not like Emil's family.

Lotte's in her own youth group. They used to go camping too. They want to build a Jewish homeland but they had to stop meeting ages ago. Lotte came home in an awful temper one day and yelled, "We're banned! Can you believe it?"

She still sees some of her friends from the group, and when she comes home she talks nonstop about going to Palestine.

Papa says, "Be quiet, please, Lotte. Germany is our homeland and that's that."

～

"Push off, Jewboy!" snarls Konrad now, and punches Emil in the stomach.

Emil doubles over, groaning.

The gang crowds around and starts to chant, "Fight! Fight!"

I open my mouth to stick up for Emil but nothing comes out.

Emil straightens and puts up his fists, but his face, usually dark like mine, has gone as white as the ice on the river.

Konrad lets out a nasty laugh and his gang shouts even louder.

Then a whistle goes and I see our teacher, Fräulein Becker, striding across the playground, blond hair in two braids swinging around her face, cheeks red from blowing so hard on her whistle.

My legs go weak with relief.

"Time for class. Go inside, please, boys. Emil, Rudi." Fräulein Becker points to us. "Walk beside me. I need you to carry some books from the office."

Phew! Saved from the Hitler gang again.

Emil gives me a grin behind Fräulein Becker's back, but I frown at him.

Why can't he keep clear of trouble, like Hanno and I? If I see Hitler Youth I duck down a street or hide behind the garbage cans until they've gone. Hanno knows when to keep quiet, but he's really brave. He'd never run off and leave me, no matter how scary things were. Hanno and I are a team and we look out for each other.

Fräulein Becker piles our arms with books, and we follow her into class.

It's silent in the room, which is strange because usually everyone's calling out and tossing things to each other. Even stranger, Konrad and his gang are sitting in the front row, arms folded neatly on their desks, looking up at a teacher I don't recognize. The teacher has very pale skin, a bit like Konrad and his gang, and he's wearing an armband with a swastika on it.

Uh-oh! I think. *He's a Nazi.*

Emil and I dump the books onto the teacher's desk, and then the man with the swastika swipes at our bare legs with a ruler. We yelp—it really hurts—and Konrad lets out a snort of laughter.

"You Jewish boys!" shouts the teacher.

He points to the yellow stars sewn on our jackets. All Jews have to wear them now—Lotte says it's utterly despicable.

"Get to the back row and I don't want to hear or smell you again today."

I look over my shoulder at Fräulein Becker. Her face has gone very white. I can see she's feeling upset too. Fräulein Becker doesn't mind that we're Jewish.

Emil tugs my arm and pulls me to the back row. When we sit down I throw him a worried glance. But nothing gets Emil down for long. He gives me a long, slow wink.

Great! Emil always has a plan. I can't wait for recess.

2. No More School

It's the worst morning in class ever. I put my hand up to answer every single question, and the Nazi teacher never asks me once. Fräulein Becker is called away, otherwise I'm sure she would have said something. Emil keeps shaking his head at me and yawning as if to say, *Why bother?*

But I always put my hand up!

The teacher keeps asking Konrad and his gang, but they don't get one single answer right. The questions aren't even that hard.

What year did Hitler come to power?

1933. Easy.

What is the capital of Poland?

Warsaw! I want to shout, but Emil frowns at me and mouths, *Keep your head down.*

Finally, it's lunchtime, and everyone goes out. Emil holds me back so we won't get trampled on. Then we run out the door while the Nazi teacher is cleaning the board.

"Let's go!" hisses Emil, pushing me toward the school gate.

"What? Skip school?" I hiss back, eyes wide with horror.

"Call this school?" sneers Emil, waving his arm around. "This is a Hitler Youth camp now, and they don't want boys like us."

Across the playground I can see Jewish kids huddled together, trying to look invisible. The other kids are roaring around, kicking balls, and yelling rude things like "Stupid Jews!"

"But Papa would be furious if—"

"Don't tell him," says Emil.

And suddenly I think, *Why not?* I can't stand the thought of afternoon class after this horrible morning.

"Where will we go?"

"The park!" shouts Emil. "Race you!"

He shoots off through the gates, and I run after him, terrified of being left alone in the Nazi school. We run all the way to the park by the river. The linden trees that line the bank are stripped of their leaves now that it's November. They look very solemn, their branches reaching up to the cloudy sky.

Will I get into trouble? I wonder. But if Fräulein Becker isn't going to teach us anymore and the Nazis have taken over, school will never be the same for Emil and I again, will it?

Then I trip over a root and scrape my knee.

"Come on, let's get you up," comes Emil's cheery voice as he helps me over to a bench.

We sit down, and I look at my watch. It's after two and everyone else will be back in class.

Monday afternoon. Usually we do painting, and then Fräulein Becker reads to us. We're halfway through *Peter Pan*, and I've been looking forward to the next chapter.

"Do you think the new teacher will read to the class?" I ask Emil.

"No chance," he says. Then he sticks his arm in the air like a Nazi and squawks, "You will copy out Hitler's speeches *all afternoon!*"

We're laughing so much we nearly fall off the bench, so we don't see an old man coming up to us.

"You Jews!" he barks. "Get off this bench. Only Germans sit on the benches."

The man's face is red with fury, and he's pointing at the yellow stars on our jackets.

I start to apologize but Emil pulls me to my feet, pokes out his tongue, and yells, "Can't catch us, stupid old man! Come on, Rudi!"

We run and run until I can't catch my breath anymore.

Then we slow down and walk to my apartment building.

I'm about to say goodbye when Emil grabs my arm, and looking straight into my eyes, he says, "Whatever happens in Germany, Rudi, you will always be my absolute best friend."

His face, usually grinning or screwed up to make us all laugh, is more serious than I've ever seen it before.

"Of course," I say.

Emil gives me a nod and then his face relaxes into his wide grin. "See you!" he says.

As he races off, I call out, "Not if I see you first!"

~

I go down the path, in through the main door, and run up two flights of stairs to our apartment. Then I open the front door with my key. I can hear Papa, Mutti, and Lotte arguing in the kitchen.

Hanno comes down the corridor and throws himself at me. As I pick him up I whisper, "Why is everyone home in the afternoon?"

Hanno gives my cheek a thoughtful lick as if to say, *No idea, Rudi.*

I carry him down the hallway and into the kitchen.

Everyone stops talking midsentence and then Papa says, "Why aren't you at school, Rudi?"

I don't say anything for a minute, and we all stare at each other.

But I can read their minds, can't I?

They're thinking what I'm thinking.

Everything's changing for the Jews, and what on earth are we going to do?

"Rudi?" says Papa.

Then I tell him about the Nazi teacher and how school is all Hitler Youth now, and Emil and I ran away.

All Papa does is nod and ruffle my hair.

So, no more school.

Is that forever?

3. Pioneers

Friday, January 27, 1939

It's my birthday in three weeks and four days. Emil's one week older than me, and we'll be nine.

All our friends came to my party last year and Papa showed a film because Jews aren't allowed to go to the cinema anymore in Germany. The film was *Tarzan Escapes*, and it was great. My Zayde Karl was still alive then and he loved the film too. But then he died and now me and Lotte don't have any grandparents anymore. Not like Emil, who still has two *zayde*s and they both give him extra pocket money every week.

After the party, Emil and I played Tarzan all the time. We'd go down to the river and try to swing through the trees, hollering away like Tarzan. We pretended Hanno was Tarzan's chimpanzee friend. He was quite good at joining in, scrabbling up at the trunks of trees and barking.

Tarzan isn't afraid of anything. He's a superhero and that's exactly what we need in Germany, isn't it? Of course, the Nazis think that Hitler is *their* superhero, but he's more like the archvillain to us Jews.

❧

Things are getting worse. I haven't been back to school since Emil and I ran away from the Nazi teacher last November. Lotte doesn't go to school anymore either, so we're both at home all day. She studies every morning and Papa keeps telling her how well she's doing. But I find it so boring doing math and other lessons by myself, and there's no one to play with anymore.

Emil disappeared just before the end of December. Papa said he and his family have emigrated to Canada. So we've all lost our friends. Mutti and Papa used to see Emil's parents all the time.

Lots of Jews we know are leaving Germany. Mutti's two cousins and their families went to America last year. Their kids always came to my birthday parties. Papa had an older brother, my Uncle Siggi, but he was killed in the Great War. So our family is just us four these days and now with Emil gone too, who will be left to come to my party? If I'm even allowed to have one this year.

Jews aren't allowed to do anything anymore. We can't go to school or the swimming pool. Jews are only allowed to go to the shops for one hour each evening, so the lines are really long. By the time Mutti gets to the counter all the good stuff has gone. I miss chocolate and fresh bread and butter and I can't have my usual big pile of potatoes at dinnertime. Mutti never makes cinnamon cookies anymore. She can't get butter and eggs. My stomach rumbles and so does Hanno's. He's on short rations too.

Lotte's in a rotten mood almost all the time. I have to stay out of her way, which is quite difficult in our apartment. I wish we lived in a castle with battlements and a dungeon. Then Hanno and I would have loads of places to disappear to when everyone's in a bad mood.

I don't dare even take Hanno out for walks in case someone snatches him. Jews get all sorts of things taken away now. I don't know what I'd do if someone stole my little dog.

I miss Emil and all my friends at school, and Fräulein Becker. One good thing, Mutti managed to borrow a copy of *Peter Pan* from the neighbor, so at least I know how it ends. If Emil was here we could pretend to be Lost Boys and Hanno would be Nana, the dog who looks after Wendy and her brothers.

Every day I practice on Papa's bugle. He brought it home from the Great War and he's teaching me how to play. Bugles only have six notes, so you can't do lots of tunes. I'm learning the call to charge, which is really exciting but very fast. Papa can play it really well. I need loads of practice but Lotte screams at me after just a few minutes. She's so annoying.

Papa was an officer in the trenches and he says that Hitler won't turn against all those brave Jewish German soldiers who fought for the Fatherland in the last war.

"Of course he won't," I say, nodding hard.

But Lotte gives a rude snort, and then Mutti tuts at her and frowns.

Papa's bugle has some dents in it from the war and a Prussian eagle like a crest on it. He says that when the bugle was blown all the soldiers went over the top into battle. But then he goes quiet and his eyes seem to be looking into the distance, as though he is thinking about the war again.

I pick up a little cloth then and start polishing so that the bugle shines and Papa can see I'm taking care of it.

"You're a good boy, Rudi," he says, and he pats my head.

But I can't play my bugle and read my books *all* day. Time goes so slowly. I wish something exciting would happen.

❦

I keep hoping Emil will write to me. Hanno waits for letters every single day but nothing comes. Papa lost his job at the newspaper ages ago and he looks bored all the time too. He listens to the radio a lot with a frown on his face. There's only one station. It plays marching music or Hitler shouting about Jews and war and other crazy stuff.

I don't like Hitler's voice. It sounds like a wolf snarling

at my heels, trying to bite me. I cover Hanno's ears so he doesn't get scared.

❧

Lotte spends a lot of time in her room writing in her stupid diary. If I knock on her door and ask if she wants to play cards she shouts, "Go away, pest!"

She's always giving big sighs at the dinner table and moaning about her friends. "Can't I just run around to Anna's apartment, or even Hans's? He's close by," she says, but Mutti tuts and Papa shakes his head.

"It's so unfair," Lotte says in a sulky voice.

I don't say anything. There's no point.

Lotte's very clever. She reads long books and talks about science with Papa. She's always been at the top of her class and wants to be a doctor when she grows up.

"If we go to Palestine, I can start medical training as soon as I'm eighteen," she said to Papa last night, in her best wheedling voice.

That's years to go. Lotte's not sixteen until September.

Papa just shrugged as usual and Mutti stared down at some socks she was mending.

"How would we get to Palestine when we can't even go shopping?" I asked.

But no one answers my questions anymore.

When I grow up I want to be an explorer and go to the jungle to see if I can find the real Tarzan. Hanno wants to come too, and he can sniff out the right path. Maybe Emil would fly over from Canada and join us.

～

Today's Friday, and Sabbath starts when it gets dark. I help Mutti make the challah after lunch. Once the dough has risen, I roll out three long pieces and Mutti braids them.

"This is how we tie everything together at the end of the week, Rudi," she says as she works. "We put our worries and cares aside until Saturday night."

She smiles at me, but she looks even more worried today. I'm not sure whether anyone in our house is putting their worries aside. Even Hanno often gives a worried whine and looks around as if asking, *Why don't we go out anymore?*

～

As it grows dark, we all gather around the kitchen table. The lights are turned off except for a corner lamp, and Mutti lights the Sabbath candles. As she says the prayer in Hebrew I look over at Lotte, the candlelight gleaming in her eyes. Usually she ignores me but tonight she stares back.

I give her a little frown as if to say, *What's up?*

She shakes her head slightly, but she doesn't look away. That is very odd.

We have a sip of wine and a piece of challah sprinkled with salt and then Mutti dishes up soup. Looks and glances are exchanged over my head.

I'm about to ask *What's going on?* when Papa starts to speak.

"Germany has changed under the Nazis, and it's no place for Jewish children anymore," he says, and takes a mouthful of soup.

A tear trickles out of Mutti's eye and rolls down her cheek.

I stare at Lotte, but she looks down at her plate.

Hanno stirs in his basket in the corner of the kitchen and gives a little whimper. Usually we laugh and joke when Hanno whimpers, but today no one says anything.

"We have made a decision," Papa goes on.

He looks straight at me, and a shiver goes down my spine. I want to go and pick Hanno up and feel his warm body against my chest, but I don't dare move; Papa looks so serious.

"We have decided to send you, Rudi, with your sister to England," Papa continues. "You have places on a train next Tuesday morning."

"But . . . but . . ." I don't know what to say. Go away from home? Are they crazy? "What about you and Mutti? I don't want to leave home," I blurt out. "I don't speak any English and Lotte will be mean to me—"

Papa puts his hand up, and his face is so stern that I stop.

"Listen, Rudi," he says. "You have to do what I say. Mutti and I know what is best for you right now. All the

Jewish children are being sent away. You're not the only one. Lotte will be very kind and helpful to you."

"Don't worry, I'll look after you," mutters Lotte.

Well, that'll be a first, I think. *She never has any time for me.*

No one says anything. They're all looking down at their plates. They must have talked about this behind my back, I decide. They're always hiding stuff from me.

I need Hanno, I think. Getting down, I pick up my little dog and sit at my place again, clutching him to me, staring around at everyone. Hanno is never *ever* allowed at the table but no one says anything, which is even more scary, to be honest.

"Hanno and I will have to think about it," I say in a growly voice, stroking Hanno's silky ears.

Papa and Mutti exchange looks and Lotte stares at me, her eyes wide as if she wants me to read her mind or something.

Then Papa says the most awful words in the world. "No, Rudi, I'm sorry, you can't take Hanno on the train."

"What!" I almost scream out. "I'm not going away from home without Hanno, not ever, absolutely *not!*"

"My darling Rudi," says Mutti, her bottom lip trembling. "We have to put you children first. It would just be too danger-ous. The soldiers might . . . they might be very unkind to you with a dog."

I open my mouth to talk back, but Papa puts up his hand and with another very stern look says, "These are terrible times. Hanno stays here."

Tears start to trickle down my face and so Papa says in a nicer voice, "Don't worry, we'll take good care of Hanno. He'll be quite safe."

"Listen to Papa," says Lotte. "Everyone I know says the same now. We have to leave Germany." Her voice drops away, and tears well in her eyes too.

Mutti's eyes are streaming and she keeps wiping them on her apron.

Then Papa says in a brighter voice, "Look, Rudi, you're always saying how bored you are stuck at home now. This will be a great adventure."

"*Huge* adventure," puts in Mutti in a shaky voice.

"You're going to be our pioneers, going ahead and finding out everything about England before we arrive," says Papa.

"Pioneers," repeats Mutti, with a nod.

"Who will I live with?" I ask in a small voice, although I have to admit I rather like the idea of being a pioneer.

"Good people," says Papa. "We've been in touch with them by letter. Their names are Herr and Frau Evans. They live in London and they have offered to look after you until we arrive. They know how badly Hitler and the Nazis are treating the Jews. They want to help us, and we are very grateful."

"But they're strangers," I say. "Do they speak German? What if their children don't like me?" A million questions go through my head. At the bottom of it I feel so scared.

Mutti wipes her eyes again and says, "They don't have children, Rudi, so they'll spoil you. I'm sure you'll feel at home quite quickly."

I bury my face in Hanno's fur, and then I look up and say, "What about Lotte? Will she live with me, too?" Even though Lotte can be a bit mean as a big sister, I don't want to go and live with strangers without her.

"We'll see when you get there," says Papa. Then he wags a finger at me. "We expect you to behave like a good Jewish boy, so we can be proud of you. Mutti and I have to sort out our papers. Then we'll come over very quickly."

The talk turns to packing and I go off to my room with Hanno. My heart feels as heavy as a stone as I watch him turn around and around on my bed like he always does, making himself comfortable. He finally settles down, curled up, nose on his legs as if he doesn't have a care in the world. *At least my little dog doesn't know what's coming,* I think, but I don't feel even a tiny bit better.

What's the point of being a pioneer without Hanno? But then I spot a notebook and pencil I've been saving on my bedside table for writing to Emil if he ever sends me his address.

"I suppose we could make some notes," I say to Hanno. I bend my head down so that Hanno and I are touching noses. "A pioneer should write down everything useful to help Mutti and Papa when they arrive in England."

Hanno gives a little bark and puts his paw on the clean page. It leaves a gray print.

"Great start," I say, and I write:

Hanno's paw print today.
We are pioneers.
No more Hitler Youth.

4. The Journey to England

Tuesday, February 7, 1939

It's been awful since last Friday night. Every day I beg Papa
to let me bring Hanno to England. I have all sorts of really
good suggestions, like making a false bottom in my suitcase
and hiding him there, or an extra pocket on the inside of my
coat.

"He's only a little dog. I promise he'll be absolutely
silent," I keep saying.

But everyone just says no.

On Saturday morning I jammed my bedroom door with
a chair and refused to come out until they let me take Hanno.
But Papa managed to push the door open and ordered me
down to lunch.

"I'm on hunger strike," I told them.

"Well, that's no problem," snapped Lotte. "There's not
much to eat these days."

She's right, of course, as usual. Mutti still manages to make delicious food but it's mainly soup with a slice or two of bread.

I glared back at Lotte and pressed my lips together, folding my arms tightly across my chest.

Only, when Mutti's soup came I couldn't keep it up. I was so hungry. I ate everything, but I was very rude, making loud slurping sounds and spitting out green beans, which I hate. I didn't seem to get into any trouble, which felt so strange.

⌒

When I wake up in the morning it's as if some great black cloud is hanging over my room. Hanno's nose is on my legs. I just can't believe that in a few hours I'll be on a train to England without him.

Then I hear someone banging on the front door and voices in the hall downstairs.

"Rudi! Come down, quick!" Mutti calls up.

Why should I? I think, pulling Hanno under the covers with me.

"Come *on*, Rudi!" It's Lotte, leaning in my doorway, with a grin on her face. "Good news for you."

I'll bet, I think, but I have to admit I'm curious now.

I pick Hanno up and we go downstairs.

Papa is beaming at me and patting a youngish-looking man on the back.

"This is Dieter, a friend of a friend from my old job.

He's offered to take Hanno to England for you," says Papa. "Dieter's not Jewish." He gives Dieter a kind smile. "So the soldiers won't stop him. Hanno will go into quarantine for six months to make sure he doesn't have any diseases, and then he'll come out and live with you again."

I stare and stare at Dieter, who has very short blond hair and gray eyes that sort of twinkle at me.

"You can trust me, Rudi. I love dogs," says Dieter. "But I have to take him right now."

And that's it. In a second, with hardly time for a kiss goodbye, my little dog has disappeared. I'll be nearly ten when I see him again, if I ever do. What if he forgets me?

∼

After that there's no time to think about anything. We have to get to the train and Mutti makes us wear everything we can put on. Soon I'm weighed down with three sweaters and a coat two sizes too big. Mutti says I'll grow into it.

Don't they have clothes in England?

At least I can hide things under all those layers. I stuff my notebook up the sleeve of one of my sweaters and at the last minute I grab Papa's bugle. I really need something special from home. You can't see it under this stupid coat. I wish I could have hidden Hanno there too.

When will I see home again, and how will Hanno find where I'm living in England? I wonder as Lotte and I walk with Mutti and Papa to the station. It's a sunny morning and the leaves on the linden trees are beginning to bud. Normally I'd run down the street, but today I have far too many clothes on. I can hardly walk.

The station is crazy; hundreds of families are crying and hugging each other. The parents aren't allowed onto the platform, so we have to say our goodbyes at the barrier. Mutti and Papa kiss me and Lotte, and then we walk away, holding hands.

"Goodbye, my darlings, goodbye," I hear Mutti call over and over until her voice is swallowed by the noise.

My eyes fill with tears, but Lotte squeezes my hand and whispers, "Think about seeing Hanno."

That helps a bit.

We get into a carriage near the front. It's so crammed with kids I have to sit on Lotte's lap, which makes me feel really babyish.

It takes ages before the train leaves, and Lotte whispers, "What if they don't let us leave?"

"Why wouldn't they?" I whisper back.

Lotte is staring out the window at a Nazi soldier with a rifle. He catches her eye and suddenly he points the barrel straight at our window and pretends to pull the trigger.

Lotte's mouth falls open into a big round O and the soldier throws his head back, laughing.

"I hate the Nazis," I whisper. "I hope they all drown like the Egyptians in the Red Sea."

That makes Lotte grin and I feel better. *At least when I get to England I'll be in the same country as Hanno again,* I think. I still can hardly believe I won't see my darling dog for six whole months.

~

Finally, the train pulls out, but no one cheers because Nazi soldiers are patrolling the train. They come into our carriage and grab a suitcase and tip everything out onto the floor.

There's a tin whistle caught in a sock and a soldier grabs it and yells, "Everyone knows the rules! You were told to bring nothing except clothes. Who's stealing from the Fatherland?"

It's only a whistle. I don't think the Germans will starve without it.

A boy in a brown jacket stands up and says, "Sorry, sir, it was a mistake." He's shaking like the branches on the linden trees in a storm.

"*You're* the mistake, Jewboy!" blasts the soldier. Then he picks up the boy's things and throws them out the window.

I can feel the bugle pressing onto my chest and my heart is thumping like a drum. *If he searches me he might be so angry he'll throw me out of the window,* I think.

But the soldier goes away.

Imagine if I had brought Hanno, and he'd been discovered.

My chest feels as though a tight band is wound around it, stopping me from breathing.

Everyone in our car goes silent and pale with fear as we rattle on through wet fields.

I think about seeing Hanno again. *What if he only understands English when we get back together? He'll probably forget all the tricks I taught him.*

Lotte stares out of the window, and she looks very sad.

I want to cheer her up so I whisper, "Pioneers, right?"

She squeezes my knee, but she doesn't smile.

~

The train chugs on mile after mile, and I begin to feel hungry. But Lotte won't let me eat the sandwiches Mutti made in case there's no more food today. It's so hot under all my layers of clothes, and my stomach won't stop rumbling.

Last night when we sat down to our very last dinner together, Papa said, "Remember you are Jewish, wherever you live or go to school—"

"And don't eat any sausages," put in Mutti.

"Why not?" I said.

"In England all the sausages are pork," muttered Lotte. "At least we don't keep kosher."

Which is true. Papa always has black coffee after dinner because he doesn't want to mix milk and meat, and Mutti never buys pork. But we're not exactly religious Jews. Emil's papa went to synagogue every Saturday morning. We only go on the High Holy Days: New Year and the Day of Atonement.

But we all love Friday nights. Mutti lights the candles and says the Hebrew prayer. Then Papa chants the prayers over the bread and wine. We love hearing him sing. His voice is sort of quiet and deep at the same time.

Papa went over all the prayers with us again last night.

"So that you never forget them," he said, with a stern look on his face.

But what if I do forget? I couldn't help thinking. *Who will I ask in England?* Mutti said Mr. and Mrs. Evans aren't Jewish, so I can't ask them, and what should I do if they make me eat pork? I could ask Lotte but she'd probably snap at me and call me a pest.

It was all very confusing, but I didn't say anything. Everyone was very quiet and sad at the dinner table and my arms were aching for Hanno.

❧

The train goes on and on and then, ages after our normal lunchtime, it stops at a tiny station. We look out the window and see the Nazi soldiers getting off. There's a short wait before the train pulls away again, but all the soldiers are still standing around on the platform, smoking and laughing.

"Why didn't they get back on the train?" I ask Lotte.

"I think we're at the border," she says.

We all press our faces against the glass and sure enough,

a few minutes later, the train slides out of Nazi Germany and into Holland.

Lotte pushes me off her lap, throws herself to her feet, and cries out, "Now we're free. No more Hitler! No more yellow stars!"

She reaches over to the star on my coat and rips it off, and then her own. All the other kids copy her and soon there's a pile of stars on the car floor, trampled under our shoes.

I'm so excited I pull out my bugle. Before Lotte can say anything, I blow the first notes of the signal to charge. Everyone cheers and bangs me on the back.

But Lotte is frowning, and she jerks my sleeve really hard when I lower the bugle. "Are you crazy, Rudi? What if the soldiers had found that!"

"But they didn't," I say, grinning.

She stares at me for a minute, and then she can't help grinning back. She still gives me a hard punch on the arm.

Sisters!

∾

The train stops in a station. Smiling Dutch people give out hot chocolate and sandwiches and fruit. We stuff ourselves before the train sets off again.

I show Lotte my notebook. "I'm making notes for Mutti and Papa," I say.

I think she'll laugh at me, but she just says, "Good thing

the soldiers didn't find that either. You could have gotten into so much trouble."

She's right, of course, but I don't say so.

Then I write:

Only pack clothes or the soldiers will be angry.
Pull off your yellow star when you cross the
border.
The Dutch make delicious hot chocolate.

~

The train comes to the sea, and we have to take a boat to England. Then we take another train to London and come out at a station called Liverpool Street. All the kids are told to sit and wait. We have huge labels around our necks, which makes me feel like a piece of lost luggage.

Some kids are collected quite quickly but it's ages before anyone comes for us. Then a kind-looking man comes over and says he is Herr Evans—the English word for *Herr* is *Mister,* Lotte says—and we should go with him.

We have to take a bus, and Lotte whispers to me that there's no room for her at the Evanses.

"I'm going to live with a couple called the Greens nearby," she says.

"I'll be all alone with them, and I don't speak English," I whisper back, my bottom lip beginning to wobble.

"I'll come and see you as much as I can," says Lotte, but her face is very pale.

❧

It's late by the time we reach the Evanses' house. Lotte gives me a quick kiss on the cheek, and then she disappears. I stand in the hallway with my tiny suitcase, and I can feel tears again. It's all so different from our apartment in Frankfurt. There's a staircase leading upstairs but it's dark up there and looks quite scary. There's a funny smell too, a bit like our apartment before Mutti opens the windows in the morning.

But Frau Evans gives me a nice smile and, pointing to herself, she says, "Auntie Irene." Then she points to Herr Evans and says, "Uncle Don."

Auntie Irene's short and very round. She has reddish cheeks and light brown hair, which she keeps pinned up on her head. She wears a flowered apron, and she smells of disinfectant and soap. Mutti always smells of cinnamon from the cookies she makes for me and Hanno.

Herr Evans—Uncle Don—is taller than Papa but he sort of stoops, and his head is half bald and half gray hair all around the back and sides. He and Auntie Irene must be years and years older than Mutti and Papa. A bit like grandparents, I suppose. They don't have any children, Mutti said, and I can't see any pets either.

Uncle Don points to my coat, so I take it off. He raises

his eyebrows when he sees the bugle, but he doesn't say anything. Then I take off two of my three sweaters, and that makes him smile. His eyes are light gray, and they crinkle up in a kind way.

I keep the notebook in my secret place up my sleeve.

We go into the kitchen and Auntie Irene shows me where to sit, and she even lets me put the bugle on the table next to me.

Uncle Don says something in English, which I don't understand, of course, and then he puts his fist to his lips and sort of blows and points to the bugle.

He wants me to play, I think, and I nod. Papa had just started to teach me the wake-up call, so I play the first few notes and then it goes all croaky, and I stop. Uncle Don gives me an approving nod. I take my special rag out of my pocket and rub it over the bugle. I think it got a bit dusty on the train. Auntie Irene says something in a nice voice to Uncle Don. They both nod at me and smile.

Papa would be proud of me, I think, and I give a small smile back.

Auntie Irene puts down a cup of what looks like milky coffee, but when I drink some it's tea with so much milk and sugar it tastes disgusting. I only drink milk or water at home. Uncle Don is cutting some bread. At least it looks like a loaf of bread, but it's white! He puts butter and jam on a slice and gives it to me. The jam tastes nice, and I eat three slices, but when Auntie Irene wants to pour me some more tea, I put my hand over the cup and shake my head.

All the time they talk in English to each other and sometimes to me. On the train Lotte taught me *yes, no, please,* and *thank you,* but apart from those words and *tea,* which is almost the same in German, I can't understand a word. It makes me feel so lonely.

Finally, Auntie Irene takes me upstairs to my new bedroom. She helps me find my pajamas in my suitcase, and I change for bed. Then she gives me a kiss on my cheek and strokes the hair on my forehead for a minute. I like that. Mutti used to do that sometimes. Then Auntie Irene goes out and closes the door, and I'm all alone.

My new bedroom's cold, with big, dark furniture. The bed's lumpy, and the sheets are all scratchy. Nothing looks or feels or smells like home. A dog barks outside in the street, and it makes me think of Hanno's warm body resting on my legs. *How long do I have to stay here?* I think, and finally tears pour down my face. I can't hold them back any longer.

Papa's bugle is on the side table with the soft rag next to it. The rag was torn off an old shirt of Papa's. I wipe my eyes on my pajama sleeve, wrap the rag around the bugle, and then tuck it into bed with me.

Lotte would laugh, I think, but I saw her sneak Mutti's silk scarf into her pocket before we left home. So she's got something to cuddle as well.

I lie there with my arm around the bugle, and then I remember I have to be a pioneer. So I pick up my notebook and write :

They have white bread in England.
Tea must have milk and sugar or it's poisonous,
*   I think.*
Sit upstairs on the bus. It's UNBELIEVABLE!!!

5. My First Week

I don't see Lotte for five whole days. I never thought I'd miss my moany sister so much. All I want is for her tell me, *Shut up, pest!*

Every morning Uncle Don goes out at eight o'clock in blue overalls while I'm brushing my teeth. I think he goes to work, so he hasn't lost his job like Papa. He gave me a long piece of string on the second evening and helped me tie it on my bugle, so now I can sling it over my back and carry it everywhere with me.

For breakfast Auntie Irene makes me a boiled runny egg, which she puts in a tiny white cup and slices off the top. On the same plate there's toasted white bread cut up into strips. On the first morning she showed me how to dip the bread into the egg and kept saying a word I didn't understand until she found it in Uncle Don's German/English dictionary. The strips of toast are called *soldiers* in English.

Nothing's like home here. Even the toothpaste tastes funny.

Mutti made me scrambled eggs for breakfast, never a runny egg, and we had dark rye bread with *Zuckerrübensirup*. It's a yummy thick black syrup, my absolute favorite. Lotte and I used to fight over the last spoonful in the jar. But that was before the Jews couldn't get much food anymore. We haven't had *Zuckerrübensirup* for ages.

Auntie Irene gives me strawberry jam on toast, which is delicious, and I'm allowed as much butter as I want. My stomach hasn't rumbled once since I arrived in England. There's plenty of food in Auntie Irene's cupboard and the bread bin has a crusty new loaf every day.

After breakfast I look at the dictionary for a bit, which is very boring, or go out in the garden if it isn't raining. I'm allowed to practice my bugle in my room for a bit too and no one tells me off.

Auntie Irene does her housework. Then we go shopping. I take the bugle, slung on my back with the string. As we walk along I can feel it bumping as though Papa's behind me, giving me a pat like he used to do.

I think of Mutti and Papa and my darling Hanno all the time. I miss them so much. At least I'm finding out about England and making my notes for Mutti and Papa, like a good pioneer.

I like the shops. They're so different from shops in

Germany. The butcher shop doesn't have the long, fat sausages hanging from hooks. Instead there are chickens, and the sausages are shorter than my hand. Auntie Irene seems to know I don't eat pork because she only gives me chicken or fish, even when they have sausages.

There's a greengrocer and a baker and all the bread is white. There isn't one loaf of bread like our dark rye bread. It's very strange. I like the smell in the baker's but out in the street there are big red buses and trucks, making a lot of noise and spewing out thick smoke all the time. Back home in Frankfurt, our streets are much quieter and when the linden trees bloom, you can smell the thick, sweet scent all the way to school.

All the food here looks so different. The cheese is not as yellow as our cheese and they cut it from big square blocks. Even the apples don't look like *our* apples. I make notes in my head for Mutti and Papa.

The best shop is the newspaper shop. They sell cigarettes and tobacco and they also sell candy, the hard kind you can suck for ages. Every day Auntie Irene lets me choose something. I'm allowed two ounces in a paper bag, which is quite a lot really and only costs two pennies. It's so long since I had any candy, and I suck each piece slowly to make them last all day.

The candy is in huge glass jars lined up on a shelf behind the counter. I always choose something different, so I can tell

Mutti and Papa about the best ones. So far, I like a stripey black-and-white candy called a bull's-eye and another called a pear drop. Maybe I can learn English by eating candy.

Auntie Irene and Uncle Don do their best to teach me English. Every evening Uncle Don points to words in his dictionary like *bread* and *cheese* and then repeats them over and over. I'm too scared to say anything much, but I'm getting quite good at remembering and understanding. It makes me feel like an explorer meeting a whole new tribe in the jungle when I learn a new word. Sort of like an adventure, only I wish Emil was here, and Hanno, of course.

I've learned to say *bugle* in English and I even taught Uncle Don the German word *Bügelhorn*. He likes it when I teach him a word in German.

The Evanses have a piano in the front room and Uncle Don plays songs and other tunes. He's teaching me to play the English national anthem, "God Save the King." I can play the first few notes with one finger, which is good fun.

❧

But mostly I just feel homesick. All I want to do is get back on the train and go home. I don't care about Hitler or the soldiers anymore. I just want to see Mutti and sleep in my own bed again.

Everything's so different in England. It makes me feel like *I'm* from a strange new tribe. The mailboxes are *red*! They're huge and stand up on the street. Proper mailboxes should be yellow and screwed on the wall like back home in Frankfurt.

The English don't live in apartments; they live in little houses stuck together in a row. Every house has a small front garden with a fence and a gate, which must be kept shut always. If our front gate is left open by the milkman, Auntie Irene tuts and says annoyed words in English.

Inside the house there's a sitting room with the piano in it and we sit there in the evenings to listen to the radio. There's a kitchen at the end of the hall, where we have all our meals. We also have to wash in the kitchen sink and Auntie Irene gives me a bath in a tin bath once a week. It's quite good fun. The toilet is a little shed at the end of the garden but I have a pot at night under the bed, in case I need it. It's a bit creepy going down the garden to the toilet when it's dark but Auntie Irene always goes with me and waits outside for me. We have to take an umbrella when it rains.

Upstairs there are just two bedrooms. The garden at the back of the house has a strip of grass and a concrete path down one side. Along the fences there are some bushes and some green shoots sticking up from the black earth. Maybe Auntie Irene likes flowers. I don't know the names of any English flowers or even many German ones. There's also a small shed where Uncle Don keeps his lawn mower.

On the first morning Auntie Irene opened the back door and pushed me out into the garden. It was very cold and muddy on the grass so I had to walk on the path down the side. It rains all the time in England.

I didn't know what to do. There was nothing to play with and no trees to climb. I walked down to the shed and tried the door, but it was locked.

Then I heard a whistle and, looking around, I saw a boy, at least fifteen, wearing a peaked cap, leaning on the fence.

He said something to me in English, but I didn't understand, which was a shame because his face was as cheery as his whistle, and he had bright blue eyes which sort of laughed as he talked.

He seemed to understand because he pointed to himself and said, "Alec."

I nodded and said, "Rudi."

I had my bugle on my back and he pointed to it. I pulled it around and blew a few notes. That made him laugh and he saluted me like a soldier. It was great.

I look for him every morning now, but I haven't seen him again. Anyway, he won't want to play Tarzan with a little kid like me, will he?

❧

Today is Sunday. Auntie Irene has been busy putting a chicken in the oven and peeling potatoes and carrots. Uncle Don keeps saying sentences with *Lotte* in them. Eventually I realize that Lotte is coming for lunch.

Finally! I thought I'd never see her again.

The morning goes very slowly and then as the kitchen clock strikes twelve there is a knock on the door. I race down the hall, open the door, and throw myself at my big sister.

She doesn't push me away. She sort of clings to me and whispers in my ear in German how much she's missed me. It feels so good my bottom lip wobbles but I manage not to cry.

I pull her down to the kitchen and Lotte says in English, "Good morning, Mr. and Mrs. Evans. I thank you for telling me to come to the lunch."

"Good English," I mutter in German.

Lotte learned some English in school last year and anyway, she learns really quickly. *I'm so much slower*, I think with a sigh.

"You have to learn too," Lotte says back in a low voice.

I go red, and Uncle Don gives me a wink. Maybe he understands some German.

"Come and sit down, dear," says Auntie Irene, her cheeks looking hot from the cooking.

Uncle Don pulls out a chair, next to my usual place.

It's wonderful having Lotte next to me. Lunch is delicious, but I'm dying for it to be over because Lotte has promised to take me out for a walk. That means we can speak German.

Finally, we've finished all the food—including apple pie and custard, which is my favorite dessert—and Lotte says to me in German that we can go out.

I race down the hall, pull on my coat, and am at the end of the path before Lotte can stop me.

"Say goodbye, Rudi," she hisses at me in German when she reaches the gate.

I turn and call out in English to Uncle Don, who is just closing the front door. "Goodbye, Uncle Don!"

He gives me his kind smile and a nod, so that's all right.

Then Lotte takes my hand, which feels so good, although I would've hated it back in Germany. We walk off to the park at the end of the road.

"They're very nice, Rudi, aren't they?" Lotte says in German.

"Yes," I say, "but I miss Mutti and Papa and you and Hanno and Frankfurt and my bedroom . . ." The tears I've been holding back all morning come rushing out.

Lotte holds my hand and waits for me to stop, which takes ages.

Then she says in a quiet voice, "I know, Rudi. I miss home too. But Germany hasn't been safe for Jews for so long and won't be until Hitler goes."

"So why don't people get rid of him?"

"I don't know. I don't understand it either. It's madness, as Papa says. But for now we are very lucky to be here and to be safe."

"But Mutti and Papa aren't safe," I say, still feeling miserable.

"They're trying very hard to get permits to leave. Mutti wrote and said maybe they can go to Cuba. Other Jews have gone there," says Lotte, but her face is very pale.

"Why don't they just jump on a train like us and come to London?"

"It's not permitted," is all Lotte says. Then she starts to ask me all sorts of questions about my week.

I dig in my pocket and pull out a crumpled paper bag with a bull's-eye and a pear drop I've saved for her.

"Thank you, pesky little brother," she says with a grin.

That makes me laugh. Not everything has changed, has it?

"What's it like with *your* family?" I say.

Lotte shrugs. "All right, I suppose. I'm sort of like a maid. I clean up, and I get two shillings a week for my pocket money, all my food, and a tiny room at the top of the house."

I frown. That doesn't sound right. "But what about school?"

"Things are different for me, Rudi. But that doesn't matter," she says quickly.

I can see she doesn't want to talk about it anymore.

"You'll start school tomorrow, Frau Evans said," Lotte tells me. "Then you can make some friends, and you absolutely must start speaking English. I know you understand a lot."

I nod, feeling miserable again.

"Promise me."

I shrug.

"Or I'll tell Auntie Irene no more candy or dessert!"

I stare at Lotte's dark brown eyes, and then a grin appears on her face. I punch her on the arm and take off as fast as I can down the path.

"Hey, pest! Come back here!" she cries out, chasing after me.

She doesn't catch me until we reach the gate. Then she grabs me, picks me up, and swings me around like she used to when I was very little.

I squeal and kick my legs out. I haven't had so much fun since I was at home with Hanno on my bed.

I have the absolute best big sister in the world.

∿

I'm so tired at bedtime, but I still take out my notebook. Mutti and Papa are relying on me. Lotte said she'll come and see me every Tuesday after school when she has her afternoon off.

I'm very scared about school tomorrow. What if everyone hates me because I'm German? Like the Hitler Youth hate Jewish boys. What if the teacher's a Nazi? I might run away, only Emil won't be there to help me.

Is he keeping a notebook too?

I'll bet he is!

Say something in English every day.
Hot custard is better than cold.
Bull's-eyes last longer than pear drops.
English apples look different, but they taste OK.
They don't have Zuckerrübensirup in England.

6. My New School

Tuesday, March 28, 1939

A cup of tea is a nice cuppa.
Dinner is called tea.
Never eat in the street. It's rude.
A bob is a shilling, which is twelve whole
  pennies. You can buy lots of candy with
  a shilling.

I've been in England for eight weeks. I feel homesick all the time. It's like a pain in my stomach, and it never goes away. I miss Hanno so much. I don't really believe he's in England. How do I know he arrived safely? Maybe someone threw him in the sea because they don't like German dogs.

I heard Auntie Irene speaking one morning over the fence to Mrs. Benson next door. She lives with her son, Alec, the older boy with the cheery whistle. I don't think there's a Mr. Benson.

I didn't understand everything Auntie Irene said but she was talking about me, saying I was a good boy, and it was awful how Hitler was treating Jewish children. Mrs. Benson kept nodding. I think Mrs. Benson and Alec understand why I'm here.

I'm still too shy to speak much English. Most of the time I keep quiet. I don't tell anyone I'm miserable, especially not Lotte. She has a rotten time with her family, the Greens. She thought they would look after her like my family does and send her to school. But instead they make her do housework all day. It's very unfair, but she says if she refuses they might send her back to Germany. That would be very scary, and Mutti and Papa would be angry with her.

How will she become a doctor if she doesn't go to school?

❧

It was my birthday on February twenty-first, two weeks after I arrived in England. I had already missed Emil's birthday, which was the week before, and now he wouldn't be here for mine. It's the first time ever in my life Emil and I missed our birthdays together.

Mrs. Benson and Alec came to tea, and of course Lotte was there. I don't have any friends my age in England. But everyone was very kind to me, and I had some good presents.

Alec gave me a little toy dog. It was a dachshund just like Hanno.

"Thank you, Alec," I said in my shy voice.

Alec grinned and stuck his thumb in the air to say OK.

Mrs. Benson had knitted me a pair of soft brown gloves. I put them on straightaway. She gave me a smile. I could see she was pleased, so I said, "Thank you," in English too.

Auntie Irene made a huge chocolate cake with thick chocolate icing. There were nine candles, and I blew them out in one go. Everyone cheered and clapped.

"You like cake, Rudi dear, don't you?" she said, cutting me the biggest slice.

I smiled and said, "Please, yes."

She gave me a nod. Auntie Irene's always happy if I say something in English.

The cake tasted wonderful. The grown-ups ate with little forks like Mutti did back in Frankfurt. But I picked up my slice and bit straight into it. I got icing on my nose, and everyone laughed.

Lotte frowned a bit and handed me her handkerchief to clean my face.

But Alec picked up his slice in both hands and took an absolutely huge bite, his eyes grinning away.

It's nice to have another boy to joke around with even though he's six years older than me. Girls just aren't the same.

Uncle Don gave me a pencil box for school. He'd wrapped it in about a million layers of newspaper and brown paper and even a bit of flowery wallpaper, so it looked enormous. We all laughed as I unwrapped and unwrapped for ages. There were a really good eraser and two brand-new pencils inside.

"Let me know when they need sharpening, eh, lad?" said Uncle Don. He always calls me lad, which is a kind word for *boy* in English. I like it.

The Evanses don't have any children or grandchildren or even any nephews and nieces. It's just them, which is a bit lonely, I think. So they're sort of practicing on me. Lotte and I think they're doing quite well.

Lotte made me a card with a big black 9 on the front.

"I don't earn enough to buy you a present yet, Rudi," she whispered to me in German.

She only earns two shillings a week and has to buy everything she needs with that, including stamps to write to Mutti and Papa in Germany. I think her family is very mean and I wish so much that she could come and live with me. But the Evanses only have two bedrooms, so it's impossible, Lotte says.

It was a nice afternoon, but I couldn't help thinking how different it was from my parties back home in Germany.

∽

My school's nearby and I walk by myself just like in Frankfurt, but it's very lonely without Emil. My teacher, Miss Cotton, is very kind, just like Fräulein Becker. She wears her hair in a bun, not in braids like German women.

They don't have any Nazi teachers. Lotte told me there

aren't any Nazis in England. The English don't like them. So I shouldn't worry about it anymore. I hope she's right.

Miss Cotton tries to get me to speak English, and I understand quite a lot now. But the other kids laugh at my accent, so I don't speak.

Then today in the playground a boy kicks a ball near me. I pick it up and hold it out to him.

"Thanks, mate," the boy says. "You the kid from Germany?"

He has a grubby face and his clothes are a bit torn, but he speaks in a sort of interested voice.

I nod, and then I think, *I must speak, I absolutely must.*

"Me, Rudi," I say, and point to my chest.

The boy grins and says, "Me, Sidney. Wanna play Tarzan?"

Just like Emil!

We run around the playground, whooping and yelling, "Me Tarzan! Me Tarzan!"

Some of the other boys join in. It's like being back in school in Germany before the Hitler Youth took over. Emil would have loved it.

"Come on, Rudi, mate," Sidney keeps calling out, and the others shout my name too.

We play Tarzan all playtime. It's amazing.

When the whistle blows, the other kids pull me into the line and one whispers, "Stand next to me, Rudi."

Back in class Sidney asks Miss Cotton if he can sit next to me.

Miss Cotton smiles and says, "Yes, of course, Sidney. Now, Rudi"—she gives me a serious look—"I want you to speak English with Sidney every day. I know you understand."

"Yes, Fräulein Cotton," I say, and I give her a polite bow like boys do in Germany.

Sidney bows too. Then all the boys stand up and bow to each other, and we all nearly fall over laughing. It's great!

~

When school is over everyone goes out of the school gate. Instead of ignoring me, lots of kids call out, "See you tomorrow, Rudi."

Sidney walks off with me, and I really want to play some more with him, so I say, "Park, Sidney?"

"*Ja*, Rudi." Sidney gives me a big grin.

Sidney's speaking German! That's so great I nearly jump for joy. *Maybe he wants to learn more,* I think.

"I have *Hund*," I tell him.

"*Hund?*" he says with a frown, looking puzzled.

I give a bark.

"Oh, you've got a dog," says Sidney. "What's his name?"

"Hanno." But I don't know how to say *quarantine*.

We run off to the park. Sidney's about my height and quite skinny, but he's strong and climbs trees even better

than Emil. We find a park bench and jump on and off, playing Tarzan. Two women walk past, but they don't tell me
off. Jews don't wear those nasty yellow stars here, so no one
probably knows who we are, do they?

~

Lotte told me not to tell anyone I'm Jewish. It's safer. But
when we're alone she talks about being Jewish back in
Germany,

"On Friday nights, even if I have to work, I think about
Mutti lighting the candles," she said once.

"Hanno always sneezed at the smell from the wick," I
said with a grin.

Lotte grinned back. "That's right, and Papa gave us a sip
of wine. I don't think English children drink wine."

"Uncle Don likes beer."

"It's not the same. Papa said the prayer in Hebrew over
the wine. Do you remember it?"

She recited the prayer and made me say it with her. I
stumbled over some of the words, but I could hear Papa's
voice in my ear.

" . . . *borei p'ri hagafen,*" we finished together.

"You must never forget we're Jewish, Rudi. Never," said
Lotte, swinging me around to face her.

Her dark eyes were very serious. I gave her hand a
squeeze to show that I was really listening.

~

To be honest, I don't think Sidney would care very much if he knew I was Jewish. He's a really great friend.

"Tarzan's the strongest man in the world," he yells to me now, and throws himself up on the wide branches of an oak tree. Oaks are thicker and taller than linden trees.

"*Ja!*" I yell back.

We play until it's time to go home, and Sidney comes with me.

When we arrive at the front garden, Auntie Irene is standing on the step.

"Sidney, friend," I say. "Nice cuppa tea?"

I thought Auntie Irene would be pleased with my English.

But instead she frowns at Sidney and says, "Not today, dear. I think you'd better go home now."

Sidney gives a shrug and says, "See ya tomorrow, mate," and he disappears.

Auntie Irene goes into the kitchen with me, saying, "I'd rather you didn't play with that boy, Rudi dear. He comes from a very poor home, and you could catch lice and all sorts of diseases from him. All right?"

I nod, but I don't really understand. Sidney's clothes are not very clean, but who cares?

Then the doorbell rings. It's Lotte. Tuesday is her afternoon off, and she always comes to see me.

"We will go to the park, Rudi," Lotte says with a smile.

She always speaks English in front of the Evanses, and Auntie Irene gives her an approving nod.

Lotte always takes my hand as if I'm too small to walk on my own, but I quite like it. Her hand's warm like Mutti's, and I swear she smells of cinnamon too.

We speak German only when we're together.

I tell her about Sidney and the playground and everyone bowing in class, which makes her laugh.

"But Auntie Irene says I can't be his friend. It's not fair," I finish.

"You can be friends with Sidney at school, but don't bring him home. You don't want to go against the Evanses," says Lotte with an anxious look on her face. "You need them on your side, don't you? Especially if they're going to take Hanno as well."

That makes me feel quite scared. Lotte's right. I need to be really, really nice all the time at home so that Hanno's looked after when he comes out of quarantine.

❧

I've been missing Hanno so much and there's still months and months to wait. But if I can't bring home my friends from school, will Auntie Irene and Uncle Don want Hanno to live with us? They never say anything to me about my dog, except once when they showed me a nice basket they have ready for him. If only they knew what a special little dog my Hanno is, I know they'd love him as much as me. At least Hanno won't be wearing torn clothes, like Sidney.

Don't speak German in the street or the
    police will arrest you.
Never say anything in Germany is better.
Look out for lice.
Never tell anyone you are Jewish.

7. Hanno Comes Home

Wednesday, July 12, 1939

It's nearly teatime, and I've been standing out on the street since I got home from school. I've slung my bugle on my back for good luck.

Hanno's coming home today!

He's finished quarantine. He's healthy, and very soon he'll be free. Will he still know me?

∞

"Bring him over to mine tonight, mate," said Sidney at school. He's nearly as excited as me. "The building next to the canal. Ask anyone, they'll show you the door."

"*Ja*," I said.

Sidney likes it if I speak German. He's picking it up very quickly. He says *gut* and *Fräulein* and *nein* and his accent's quite good. He says it'll be useful in the war.

∞

"Any sign, Rudi, love?"

Auntie Irene has come down the path. She's got a

dishcloth in her hand, and she's raised the other hand to shade her eyes and look down the street.

I shake my head.

An air raid warden goes past on his bicycle. He has a whistle around his neck and a tin helmet with ARP in thick white letters on it. Uncle Don says he'll boss us around when the Germans bomb London.

What will it be like when bombs fall on us? Will it be like when a branch of one of the trees broke in the park one day and Emil and I jumped out of the way just in time? That was very scary but tree branches don't explode like bombs. Sidney says if a bomb hits our house the roof will fall in. I'll have to try to be brave so that Hanno doesn't get too scared.

The grown-ups talk about war all the time now as if it will start tomorrow. Uncle Don works in a factory, and I heard him telling Auntie Irene that they're changing all the machines so they can make spare parts for tanks and armored cars.

When we go shopping Auntie Irene gives me a big bag, and she fills it up with extra cans and packets of food.

"For my stock cupboard," she tells the shopkeeper, and he nods.

"Everyone's doing the same," she says when we walk home.

The bag's so heavy I can hardly carry it, but I can't help

noticing that Auntie Irene has bought some cans of dog food too. So Hanno won't go hungry.

Uncle Don's always shaking his fist at the radio these days and saying, "That Mr. Hitler's a right lunatic."

He looks just as angry as Papa back home when *he* heard the news on the radio.

I don't know what to say.

Lotte says, *Keep quiet.*

~

A big white van turns onto the road and drives down, stopping right in front of me. When the engine turns off there's the sound of dogs barking.

"Here we are," says the driver. He opens the back and brings out a chocolate-brown dachshund. "Yours?" he asks.

"Hanno!" I cry out, and the man drops a little dog into my arms.

The dog has a funny stale smell and doesn't move at all. *Is it Hanno?* I can't help thinking. Then he twitches the end of his nose and gives a sneeze.

"You *are* Hanno," I whisper in German, and my lovely, velvety little dog licks and licks my face like he always used to do.

I close my eyes and for a second I almost think I'm back home, Mutti standing next to me with her sweet cinnamon smell.

But there's only Auntie Irene.

"What a nice doggie," she says. "Bring him inside."

In the kitchen Hanno gobbles up a bowl of scraps. Even Auntie Irene laughs and fills his bowl up a second time. I can't help wondering if they've fed him properly all these months. I can feel his ribs when I cuddle him. Hanno was always such a nice round sort of dog back in Germany.

After Hanno has finished eating, his eyes begin to close a bit.

"Take him upstairs and show him your room, lovey. Looks like he could do with a bit of a sleep."

"Yes, thank you," I say. Auntie Irene gives me a nice smile and pats my head. I really need her to like Hanno even if that means I have to speak English more.

I pick Hanno up and carry him upstairs. Once he's on the bed, my cold, lonely room seems much more like home for the very first time.

"You can sleep on my legs tonight," I tell Hanno.

He turns around and around, finding his comfortable spot, and then he gives another sneeze. I laugh out loud, and he gives me one of his short barks, which means, *Let's play, Rudi!* He doesn't seem sleepy anymore, so we chase each other around the bed like we used to do in my old bedroom in Frankfurt.

I feel so happy inside and all over. Hanno and I won't *ever* be separated again.

"Come on, boy," I say. "Let's go and find Sidney. He's my best friend, just like you."

I sling my bugle over my back, pick Hanno up, and carry him downstairs. Uncle Don bought a brand-new leash for Hanno last week. I clip it on before opening the front door. We go down the garden path and jog all the way to the canal.

Sidney's apartment building is set around a courtyard piled high with rubbish, which smells really bad. For a moment I hesitate. Maybe Auntie Irene was right about Sidney and his family, and I shouldn't go and visit them.

Then someone taps me on the shoulder. I turn around to see a man in a flat cap, shoulders hunched up.

"You looking for someone, nipper?"

"Sidney Scudder," I say in my best English accent.

The man narrows his eyes for a second. I think, *What if he gets mad because I'm German?*

Then the man gives a nod and says, "Second floor, end of the landing."

I mumble, "Thank you," and walk away quickly.

The stairs are wet and slippery, and it's dark climbing up. At the end of the landing on the second floor I find a door with peeling black paint.

What would Auntie Irene or Lotte say if they saw me here? I wonder, but I knock anyway.

After a minute Sidney appears and says with a grin, "Is that Hanno? Smashing."

We go inside and along a corridor to a room. I think it's the kitchen, but there's no sink, just a table and a couple of rickety chairs and a shelf with some cups and plates.

"This is Mum and Baby Tom," says Sidney.

A woman with a thin face is sitting in the corner holding a very tiny baby wrapped in a ragged shawl. The room is cold and smells a bit.

But Sidney's mum gives me a kind smile and says, "Hello, dearie. Nice cuppa tea?"

"We ain't got no milk," mutters Sidney.

"Good," I say.

Sidney gives me a grin and boils a kettle on a single gas ring.

"This is the best cup. It's got roses on it," he says.

He hands me a cracked china cup with no handle, but the tea tastes much better than Auntie Irene's sweet milky tea. He puts down a bowl with water for Hanno and I settle him on the floor, even though it's rather dirty.

"Sidney tells me your mum and dad are still in Germany," says Sidney's mum. "You must miss them ever such a lot, lovey. Do you have a picture of them?"

"Mu-um," says Sidney with a frown.

I don't mind. I like talking about my family.

Auntie Irene and Uncle Don have seen my pictures and some that Lotte brought too. They say lots of nice things. I know they would like Mutti and Papa very much.

I keep a photo in my notebook in my pocket. I take it out and say, "Mutti," pointing to her face.

"Oh, yes, Mummy," says Sidney's mum.

"Papa and Lotte," I say, pointing to them.

"Daddy and big sister. What a lovely family you got, dearie. Lucky you, eh, Sid?"

I think my chest will burst with pride. Sidney looks pleased too.

"Sidney has nice good family," I say in my best English.

Two bright red points appear on Sidney's mum's cheeks and she says, "Oh, ain't that nice, eh, Sid? What a lovely friend you got here. You make sure you take good care of him. That Mr. Hitler, he ain't no good, eh, Rudi?"

I give a big frown and nod hard so she'll know I'm not a Nazi.

"You should play your bugle for Mum," says Sidney, and his mum raises her eyebrows.

I duck my head but I pull my bugle off my back and play a few notes. Hanno gives a couple of loud barks, like he did back home when I played, and Sidney's mum claps when I stop.

"That's clever, ain't it, Sid?" she says, rocking Baby Tom, and Sidney looks all sort of proud.

He's as good a friend—they say *mate* in English—as Emil, which is lucky for me and Hanno.

"Now, you boys take that dog for some fresh air down

the canal," says Sidney's mum. "Then you see Rudi safely home, Sid. There's a good boy."

"Righto, Mum," says Sidney.

We run out of the apartment, Hanno trotting beside me on his leash, and down to the towpath alongside the canal. A mother duck floats past, and we count nine fluffy babies. The sun is still high in the sky and there are blue and yellow wildflowers in the grass. I can't help thinking that the linden trees would be thick with leaves along the banks of the River Main back home in Frankfurt.

But home isn't the same anymore now that Hitler has taken over. All the good Germans are leaving or in prison, Lotte says. Papa writes her long letters about how horrible things are in Frankfurt and how good it is we are safe in London.

Sidney's mum understands I'm a good German, doesn't she?

"Apple?" I say to Sidney, and take two out of my pocket.

"Smashing," says Sidney, and he crunches his down, swallowing the core and everything.

I keep Hanno on the leash so he won't fall in the water. He rolls in the grass as if he hasn't been outside since we lived in Germany.

"Nearly the summer holidays," Sidney says. "We can take him out every day, eh, Rudi, mate?"

"*Ja*," I say, and patting Hanno's back, I say, "*Braver Hund.*"

"*Braver Hund*," repeats Sidney. "I bet that means *Good dog*."

"*Ja*. You have so good German," I say.

"Race you," says Sidney, and I run after him, the bugle bumping on my back and Hanno barking behind us, just like back in Frankfurt with Emil.

❧

After tea we sit in the sitting room, Hanno on my lap. It's quiet except for the crackling of the fire and the clicking of Auntie Irene's knitting needles. I'm planning all the games me and Hanno could play over the summer with Sidney.

"He's a quiet little thing, isn't he, Don?" says Auntie Irene, smiling over at Hanno.

Hanno gives his little sneeze.

Uncle Don doesn't say anything. He's reading the newspaper. I can see the headlines.

WAR PRODUCTION DOUBLED
FACTORIES TURN OUT HUNDREDS OF
SPITFIRES

England's getting ready for war with Germany. Everything's beginning to change, like back home in Germany, only in England they don't seem to be angry with the Jews.

Uncle Don has been digging a very big hole in the back garden for our air raid shelter. Hanno and I have been helping. Last week a big truck delivered the shelters to our street. They're made of corrugated iron (I don't know how to say that in German, I had to ask Lotte) and each shelter has six huge pieces. Alec Benson from next door came over to help Uncle Don put it together. I passed the screws and held the hammer.

"Everyone has to help with the war effort, eh, Rudi?" says Alec with a grin.

He works at the London Zoo and loves animals. He's always dropping bits of food over the fence to Hanno.

Uncle Don paused for a moment and said, "It'll be all hands on deck once the bombing starts," and he raised his eyebrows toward me.

I nodded firmly back and made Hanno nod too, so they would know that we don't like the Nazis.

Auntie Irene keeps saying how damp and muddy it will be in the shelter, and I don't think it looks very cozy. But Alec and Uncle Don seem to think it will be the only safe place when the bombing starts. We've all got gas masks now too. Auntie Irene hung them up in the hall so we always know where they are.

Everyone in Great Britain has them, Sidney says. The government thinks Germany might drop gas on the cities. But no one says whether the shelters can keep out gas.

I keep quiet, like Lotte says.

Now as I sit staring into the fire, Hanno gives another little sneeze and Auntie Irene says, "Hanno won't be any trouble in the war, will he, Don?"

Uncle Don snaps his paper shut and says, "Not until the bombing anyway."

I feel Hanno tense on my legs, and I stroke his back.

"Well," Auntie Irene goes on in her comfortable voice, "we don't know there will definitely be a war."

Uncle Don doesn't say anything else.

You see, I think as loud as I can, hoping that Hanno can read my mind. *Nothing to worry about.*

~

I can hardly wait to go to bed and lie down with Hanno's warm body across my legs.

After Auntie Irene has come up to say good night and turn out the light, I pull my flashlight and notebook out from under my pillow.

"I'm still making notes for Mutti and Papa," I whisper to Hanno, opening the last page for him.

Always carry your gas mask.
Make sure your flashlight has good batteries.
Don't talk about the war to Uncle Don, it
    makes him worried.

Hanno licks the page and smudges a bit of my writing.

"Great," I say. "You can help me."

He gives a little whimper and settles down as I push everything back under my pillow.

We lie still for a little while, Hanno's nose over my legs and me stroking his soft ear and jaws. Sidney loves being with Hanno as much as me, and his mum is so nice. She might be poor, but she thinks I have a nice family.

Papa always said you should judge someone by what they do and what they say, not by their money or religion or country.

"If more German people listened to their hearts instead of Hitler's stinking speeches," he said, "then they would never turn on the Jews."

Papa wouldn't mind me being friends with Sidney, I know it.

8. Sausages and Campfires

Tuesday, August 15, 1939

"Over here, Rudi," Sidney calls out to me from the bridge on the canal.

I whistle to Hanno, who's nosing around in the bushes, and we jog over.

"What are we doing today?" I ask.

"Neville said the Scouts are camping in a field up the canal," says Sidney. "They're making fires and cooking sausages. Neville's mate, Miles, is gonna be there. They might let us join in."

Scouts? Aren't they like Hitler Youth? I think.

I bend down and fiddle with Hanno's collar, my bugle falling around my neck. Neville's twelve. He's Sidney's big brother, and he's good fun. Sidney and I have been playing outside all summer and sometimes Neville joins us. I'm teaching him to play the bugle but he's not very good and mostly he can't get the notes out.

But what if this Miles is a bully like Konrad Müller and his Hitler Youth gang?

"Ain't you hungry?" says Sidney, shoving his hands in his pockets. "I'm dying for a sausage."

I shake my head. I had toast for breakfast and Auntie Irene always packs up sandwiches for me because we stay out until teatime. I share them with Sidney. He never has any food with him.

Hanno has found a rabbit hole and is digging away, earth flying in all directions.

I watch him for a minute and then I say, "What if Scouts not like a dog in the tent?"

"*Nein,*" says Sidney, and he laughs.

We usually laugh together when Sidney speaks German, but today I don't feel like it.

"Please, Sidney, do not say I am German boy . . ." I hesitate and then I say, "Or Jewish boy."

Sidney gives me his wide grin and says, "Don't worry, mate. I'll keep quiet, promise. Come on!"

Then he runs off up the towpath, Hanno racing after him. There's nothing I can do except follow and hope for the best.

❧

We jog beyond the broken old factories that line the canal bank and then past some trees. A crow swoops overhead, and the sky is as blue as the sea, but my head is full of worried thoughts.

Suddenly Sidney skids to a halt and waves to someone. Squinting in the sunlight, I see Neville up ahead calling to us. Down the canal bank there is a field with six white tents pitched in a large circle. Smoke spirals up to the sky from the middle. Everywhere boys run around, carrying things and shouting to each other. They're all older than me and much bigger. They wear green shirts and khaki shorts.

"Hitler Youth," I whisper to myself. My legs turn to water.

Before I can gather Hanno in my arms and make a run for it, Neville is yelling, "Over here!"

Neville and Sidney run off, Hanno racing as fast as he can after them. He wants a sausage too.

I stay on the canal bank, my legs wanting to run away, but nothing would make me leave Hanno in the hands of the enemy. So I walk down the slope into the camp. I've swung the bugle around to my chest and I'm clutching it as if Papa could save me somehow.

I catch up as the others are talking to a big boy, taller than Neville, with square shoulders and long, chunky legs.

"Miles, this is our mate, Rudi," says Neville.

Miles gives me a nod. "Can you play that?" he asks, pointing to the bugle.

I nod but he just shrugs.

Then he and Neville walk off between the tents with Sidney. Hanno is running about yapping in his excited way.

In the middle of the circle a huge campfire is roaring away. A group of boys are cooking sausages over the fire on sticks. Another group are buttering bread, and a kettle is whistling on a smaller fire to one side.

"This is Scout Leader," says Miles, bringing us over to a tall young man.

The leader wears a khaki shirt and shorts. He has light brown hair and eyes that seem to stare right through me.

Here we go, I think. *Now the trouble starts.*

But when the leader speaks, his voice is deep and firm and—well—kind at the same time.

"Welcome, boys," he says. "Come and join us for lunch."

His eyes settle on me.

I feel all flustered and hot so I mutter in my best English, "Thank you." Then without thinking, I bow.

The leader looks startled, and Neville says with a grin, "That's what German boys do."

Sidney gives him a shove, and Neville shouts back at him.

Now I'm in for it, I think. I glance over my shoulder, looking for Hanno and the quickest way to get out and back to safety.

But the leader is saying something to me. "Did you come on the train from Germany?" His eyes are fixed on me, but they're crinkled in a nice way.

I take a deep breath, and I nod.

"Then I am *extra* pleased you have come to join us today," he says.

He turns away and that's that.

Suddenly I have a million new friends. Someone starts a soccer game and Sidney pulls me over to join in. I very nearly—almost—score a goal!

Everyone cheers and calls out my name just like at school when Sidney became my friend. Hanno zips up and down on the edge, and people keep running over to pat him.

"He's our mascot, eh, Rudi?" calls out Miles, and I nod, feeling very proud of my little dog.

When the food is ready, I give the leader my sandwiches and apples to share and he nods approvingly.

The Scouts hand around sausages stuffed between huge slabs of bread. Sidney has one in each hand and he doesn't know which one to bite first.

The leader says to me quietly, "I know you can't eat pork sausages, Rudi, because you are Jewish, right?" He raises an eyebrow at me.

I nod back, my cheeks bright red, and wipe some dust off my forehead.

"Don't worry," he says, patting me on the back. He hands me one of the cheese sandwiches. No one else takes any notice.

Hanno and I sit around the campfire with Sidney and Neville and the Scouts, singing songs and eating. Scout Leader points to the bugle and asks me to play, so I play the wake-up call and the call to charge. All the boys cheer and some of them even salute like Alec Benson.

Then we all stand up and sing "God Save the King" and I join in with almost the whole first verse. Sidney gives me a nod and I think how proud Papa would be.

Emil would love the Scouts, I can't help thinking. We were so jealous when the Hitler Youth went off camping and left out us Jewish boys. English Scouts aren't mean. They include everyone.

When it's time to leave, the leader calls us over and says, "Come and visit us anytime, and next year you will be old enough to join the Scouts. Everyone will have to do their bit when this war starts . . ." He raises his eyebrow at me again.

I give a firm nod back so that he'll know I'm not a Nazi.

"The Scouts will be needed too," says the leader.

❧

That night in bed, Hanno's nose resting on my legs, I write in my notebook:

Don't eat sausages, ask for cheese instead.
Scouts are nothing like Hitler Youth.
Be ready to do your bit. The English like that.

9. A Deep, Dark Hole

Monday, August 28, 1939

Only one more week until the summer holidays end and school starts again.

Or the war begins.

I have to carry my gas mask all the time now, and everyone says we'll be bombed. The windows have blackout curtains so the bombers won't see lights at night, and the air raid wardens shout at anyone who leaves them open. Uncle Don puts the news on every evening and shakes his fist at the radio. Auntie Irene tells him to calm down.

I don't say anything. I just stroke Hanno so he doesn't get too scared. It's so hard to know what the war is going to *be*. It makes me scared to think about bombs dropping and guns going off. What if the Nazis invade England like they invaded Czechoslovakia? What will happen to me and Lotte, and will they decide Hanno is a Jewish dog and be mean to him too? Auntie Irene tells me not to worry too much about the war and says they will look after me and keep me safe.

But they don't really know anything about Hitler and the Nazis, do they? Not like me and Lotte, who had to leave our home to be safe.

And Hanno too.

Sidney and I go back to the Scout camp twice more, and it seems now that people are always calling out to me when I walk through our streets. I still don't like speaking English much, but I manage a few words, and everyone loves it when I play a few notes on my bugle.

Mostly Hanno speaks for me, barking and jumping up at our new friends. They feed him treats, which he loves, of course.

Hanno and Sidney and I have gone miles and miles over the holidays. We pretend we're intrepid explorers and we've found a new land no one knows anything about. We call it Zanland after Tarzan and we've made up our own language, Zanlandish, which is a mixture of German and English. I made up a little tune on the bugle that Sidney calls the Zanland National Anthem and when I play he sings "God save Zanland."

~

"*Ja*—hey!" I call out to Sidney this morning in Zanlandish when I see him on the towpath.

Hanno is sniffing around at an old rabbit hole.

"*Bitte*—better keep an eye on your dog," says Sidney, using one of our special words.

"Why?"

"The grown-ups are getting rid of pets because of the war. They're talking about it everywhere." He shakes his head as if it's all crazy.

I don't understand but I grip Hanno even tighter. *Auntie Irene likes Hanno,* I tell myself, *and he's never been any trouble.*

I forget about Sidney's words and even the war as we play all day, making up games in Zanland. I wish the summer could go on forever and ever.

∞

It doesn't matter what time Sidney gets home. His mum isn't very strict. But I'm late getting back for tea again.

Uncle Don is already sitting in his place, buttering a piece of bread.

There's a bowl of scraps for Hanno and he starts to eat as soon as I put him down.

"Sorry, late," I murmur as I sit down.

Uncle Don tuts a bit, but Auntie Irene gives me her kind smile.

"Eat up, now, lovey," she says.

There are hard-boiled eggs and salad and thick slices of bread and butter. I can see a fruitcake on the side as well. Auntie Irene knows I love cake.

Hanno finishes before anyone else, as he always does, and gives a little whine. I start to laugh.

Uncle Don puts his nose over the paper and smiles a bit, but then he says, "Growing dogs eat rather a lot of food, don't they?"

I can't help thinking, *Does he think I eat too much because I'm a growing boy?*

Auntie Irene pushes my plate toward me. I eat a bit more, but it sticks in my throat. I can hardly swallow the cake when she cuts me my usual big slice.

∽

After tea we sit in the sitting room, but I make Hanno stay in his basket in the kitchen. *Maybe Uncle Don will forget about him eating lots of food if he doesn't see him,* I think.

I can't wait for bedtime, but as I'm brushing my teeth I hear voices raised down below and Hanno's name. I creep downstairs and listen from the bottom step. Uncle Don is saying something about the neighbors.

" . . . all putting their dogs down now," he says. "They're saying they can't feed them once rationing starts." His voice sounds quite sad, really.

"Hanno's only a little dog, and you know how Rudi loves him," says Auntie Irene.

They're quiet for a while and I sit there holding my breath, feeling really scared.

Then Uncle Don says, "Look, the boy goes away next week. I think we should take the dog to the vet tomorrow and have him put down. Get it over with; give the boy time to come to terms with the loss before he goes off. We did the right thing taking in the little lad—"

"Oh, yes!" cuts in Auntie Irene.

"But everyone's worried about food running out once the war starts. The government will bring in rationing, and then how on earth will we feed ourselves, let alone a dog? It's the kindest thing to do," finishes Uncle Don.

Auntie Irene gives a sigh, and then I hear footsteps and flee back to bed.

I lie under the covers, shivering with shock. *I was right! I'm being sent away because I'm German and Uncle Don is going to put Hanno down a deep, dark hole to starve to death.*

What on earth can I do?

I think and think. Then I have a great idea. I'll take Hanno to Sidney's and ask him to hide him for me. I can't waste any time; I'll go tonight.

It's already late and very dark outside. The thought of walking in the empty streets all by myself really scares me.

But I must be brave to save Hanno's life, I tell myself. *I can't let him down.*

～

I wait until the house is quiet. Then I sling my bugle around my back for luck and creep downstairs carrying Hanno. I have to push the big bolt on the back door. It makes a terrible scraping sound, and my heart leaps into my mouth. But no one comes. I leave a bucket propping the door open so I can get back in.

I pick up Hanno and run out of the back garden, down the alley to the road, and then all the way to the canal, the bugle bumping away on my back. Sidney's building looms up like a ghostly castle. A door slams, and a man shouts something rude. I shrink back against a wall. Drops of cold water fall down my neck. Then something scurries over my shoe, and a rat runs across the courtyard.

I nearly scream. I would run home if my legs weren't wobbling with fear.

But Hanno sneezes in my arms, and I think, *I can't turn back. I'm his only hope.*

I run across the yard and through the doorway and up to Sidney's front door. I knock and knock until Sidney's mum appears, carrying Baby Tom.

"It's very late, dearie. What're you doing here?" she says.

"*Bitte*, Sidney?" I'm so scared I forget to speak in English.

"Come in," she says, turning back into the flat.

Sidney is in the kitchen with Neville.

"What's up, mate?" asks Sidney.

I tell the whole story. They all listen.

When I finish, Sidney and Neville exchange looks, and then Sidney says, "*Put down* don't mean in a hole, Rudi, mate. It means *kill*—at the vet. Lots of pets are being killed now, like I said at the canal. But don't worry. Me and Neville know what to do."

Great! Sidney has a plan just like Emil always did.

"Go and see Tilly," says Sidney. "She lives down your street, Number Twenty-Seven. Got it?"

"*Ja, siebenundzwanzig,* twenty-seven," I repeat in German and English.

"Say I sent you. She's got a hideout for pets in the woods," Sidney says.

Hanno sneezes, which makes everyone laugh.

Sidney's mum says Hanno could stay with them for now. I'll have to tell Auntie Irene and Uncle Don that he's run away or something.

I'm not looking forward to that bit.

Neville and Sidney walk me back home and I sneak in without anyone seeing me.

Just before I fall asleep I think, *Sidney and I are like Tarzan looking after the animals. Maybe we could call the hideout Zanland.*

∾

The morning after I've left Hanno at Sidney's, I say my dog has run away and I can't find him anywhere. Uncle Don seems sad and worried.

But the truth is, Uncle Don wants to kill Hanno, like Sidney and Neville said.

"I look all places," I say, and I put a big piece of bread in my mouth so I can't speak anymore.

10. Saving Hanno Again

Wednesday, August 30, 1939

When I saw Lotte yesterday on her afternoon off, she was the angriest I've ever seen her.

"How could you be so foolish?" she hissed at me in German as we walked through the park.

She was walking so fast I almost had to run to keep up.

"Going out at night all by yourself. Anything could have happened to you."

She stopped as a couple went past pushing a baby carriage, but as soon as they'd gone, she went off again like a steam train.

"What if you'd met a bad man or fallen in the canal? Imagine how the Evanses would feel after everything they've done for you!"

"I did it for Hanno," I sobbed, tears running down my face.

But Lotte didn't comfort me. "You have to think about yourself now, Rudi. You're a Jewish German boy stuck in this country, which is about to go to war with Germany. What would you do if the Evanses abandoned you?"

I couldn't speak because I was crying so much. In the end I think Lotte felt a bit sorry for me.

"I suppose we could go and see if this girl, Tilly, is any use," she muttered, but she still sounded mad at me. "Let me do all the talking, right?"

I nodded and her shoulders dropped a bit, so I could see she was a bit calmer.

～

We went to collect Hanno from Sidney. His mum pulled out an old sack and said perhaps we should put Hanno inside in case someone spotted us. I know Lotte was thinking of the Evanses and she said "Thank you" in her most polite voice.

Then we walked over to Tilly's house and knocked on the door. I took Hanno out of the sack because he was sneezing while we waited for the door to open. I looked all around but there was no one else in the street.

Tilly took one look at Hanno and told us to come inside, putting a finger to her lips. We ran upstairs to her bedroom, trying not to make a sound.

Once inside her room, Tilly said in a low voice, "Mum and Dad are downstairs. They mustn't know there's a dog in the house."

Lotte pulled her over to the window, and they talked

in low voices. I couldn't follow what they were saying, and then Hanno gave a sneeze.

"My dog does that," said Tilly with a grin.

Tilly's twelve. She has long, tangly sort of hair the same color as mine. I think she's really nice, and I could see Lotte liked her too.

Tilly understood right away about saving Hanno.

"The grown-ups want to kill all the pets," she said, walking up and down with her hands on her hips and a serious look on her face. "This is the children's war. Saving the animals. You can bring Hanno to our hideout."

It was such a relief I nearly whooped for joy, but Tilly put her finger to her lips.

～

Lotte was still frowning as we walked off, but she gave me a hug, so everything really is all right.

I must be careful not to make her angry again. Mutti and Papa wouldn't like that, would they? And I definitely mustn't upset Auntie Irene and Uncle Don. There are so many things to think about, my head feels like it's spinning, but at least Hanno is safe again.

For now.

～

Back at home after seeing Lotte, Uncle Don asked me if I'd found Hanno. "I'm so sorry he's run away, Rudi. Maybe he just went out and got lost. Have you looked all along the canal?"

He sounded as though he cared about Hanno, but how could he?

❧

This morning I collect Hanno from Sidney and we go to the hideout. You would never guess it was there. It's an old hut in a clearing in a wood, beyond the canal and the old factories. It's across a field and through a thicket with millions of nettles and thorns. Grown-ups wouldn't even try to go through. It's such an amazing secret.

Tilly is busy with her dog when we arrive, so Sidney says, "Come into the hut."

It's quite dark inside and the walls are crumbling, but all over the floor are wooden crates, the tops covered with chicken wire. Inside the crates are rabbits and guinea pigs and even a tortoise. I've always wanted a tortoise.

"You tie Hanno up here at night, all right?" says Sidney. "Don't want him running off in the dark."

He shows me a bit of rope knotted around a nail on the wall.

I nod but I don't set Hanno down. How would he feel being abandoned all alone in this cold, dark hut at night?

Sidney points to a tank in the corner. "We got a baby cobra in there."

I raise my eyebrows and grin. A poisonous snake. Great!

"The grown-ups don't want to look after pets in the war and they're killing hundreds," says Sidney. "Even all the poisonous animals in the London Zoo. Freddy"—he nods toward the cobra tank—"was born in the zoo last weekend. Tilly says we're like a zoo now, so we call it the emergency zoo. Smashing, ain't it?"

"*Ja, gut,*" I say.

We go back outside and I set Hanno down. "*Sitz, Hanno,*" I say in German, but in a quiet voice. I don't want the other kids to hear me.

Hanno sits down straightaway and fixes his eyes on me as if to say, *Look how good I am.*

"*Braver Hund,*" I say, and open my hand. There's a bit of cookie sitting there. Hanno reaches up and crunches it down whole.

"Sit, Hanno, good dog," translates Sidney. "You're training him good, Rudi, mate."

There's a bowl of water in the grass for the dogs, and I put it in front of Hanno.

Then we hear a shout. "Oi, you two, what're you playing?"

It's Miles from the Scout camp, leaning against a tree, holding a homemade bow and some arrows. As we watch, he loads an arrow, takes aim, and fires. The arrow flies straight across the clearing and bounces against a tree trunk.

"Let's have a go, mate," Sidney calls out, running over.

We all have a turn with the bow and arrows. Then Sidney tells Miles all about Zanland and our Tarzan games. Miles is even better at climbing trees than Sidney. It's wonderful out here with all the kids and pets in the emergency zoo. I wish we could stay here forever.

∾

We play all day until Tilly calls us over. We have to learn SOS in Morse code, which is the warning if grown-ups come to the clearing. I blow it out on my bugle and everyone claps, which makes me go very red.

Everyone is talking and writing things down. It's too difficult for me to follow, so I go over to the thicket to keep watch.

"You're a very useful person, Rudi," calls out Tilly.

I feel my chest swell. *I wish Lotte thought I was useful, and the Evanses. Then no one would want to send me away.*

I keep my bugle on my chest and my hand on it, in case I have to blow out the warning signal. It's quiet by the thicket and Hanno is snuffling around at my feet.

Then I hear a shout. Three boys and a huge boxer dog are pushing into the thicket and calling to each other. They're big and chunky, with really mean faces.

Just like Hitler Youth!

My legs start to shake, but I know I must warn Tilly. I blow the SOS on my bugle as hard as I can. Then I run back to the clearing.

The boys chase after me, the big dog barking and tugging on his chain.

Then the biggest boy shouts, "Go on, Boxer!"

He lets go of the chain. The dog races forward and closes his jaws right around my leg. I scream and drop the bugle in a puddle.

He's going to kill me! rockets through my head, and my legs turn to water. *What if he bites my throat!*

All the kids in the clearing seem to freeze like ice statues.

Are they going to let me die? Tears well up in my eyes.

Then Tilly steps forward and cries out, "Call your dog off, Conor! Rudi's only nine."

Conor's just like Konrad Müller in the Hitler Youth.

And Tilly's really brave for a girl—as brave as Emil.

"Rudi?" says Conor. Then he spits on the ground. "That's a German name. He could be a German spy."

His gang jeers, but Conor whistles, and his nasty dog lets me go.

I limp off to the den, scooping up Hanno and cuddling him close. There are red tooth marks on my leg. That boxer dog could eat Hanno alive.

Tilly and Conor are arguing when Miles fires an arrow from his bow at Conor's dog and only just misses him.

Now they'll go away, I think.

But they don't. Instead Conor's face goes red, and he

snarls in a Nazi voice, "You trying to kill my dog? You need a right bashing!"

"You and whose army?" jeers Miles.

Sidney is yelling too, but Neville holds him back. Sidney isn't scared of anything, but he's too small to fight Conor, just like Emil could never beat Konrad Müller.

Then Conor throws himself on Miles. Miles punches Conor hard on the chest, and we're all cheering for Miles. But suddenly Conor punches Miles on the nose. Blood spurts everywhere. Then he pulls Miles's hair when he's on the ground.

"I'll knock your block off!" shouts Sidney, punching the air with his fists, but Neville won't let him go.

Conor wins, of course. Hitler Youth always win.

Conor and his dog and his gang go off and leave Miles with a bloody nose.

Everyone stands around looking miserable.

Then Tilly's friend Rosy says, "I think we should take an oath."

"Good idea," says Tilly. She swears on her dog's life she would never give away the emergency zoo.

Everyone promises, and I say, "*Ja*, Hanno."

"That's right, mate," says Sidney with a grin, and I feel a bit better.

It's time to go home. I tie Hanno up in the hut, but it's horrible leaving him to the dangers of the night. I can hear him whining and barking as I push back through the thicket with Sidney and Neville. *What if a wolf comes and eats him up? Do they have wolves in England?*

~

As I lie in bed that night, cold and lonely without Hanno to warm my legs, I wonder if I'm brave enough to go back to the den. *What if Conor comes back and kills me because I'm German?*

Then I remember Tilly saying, "This is the children's war. Saving the animals."

I have to save Hanno, don't I? So I have to be brave. I don't have a choice.

I don't want Papa to be ashamed of me when he comes over to England.

11. A Silver Shilling

Sunday, September 3, 1939

The worst thing in the whole wide world has happened.

Britain has declared war on Germany!

Now Hanno, Lotte, and I can't possibly go home, and maybe Mutti and Papa can't escape until the war ends.

Lotte said last week that I'll be sent away to the country with Tilly and her school next Tuesday because London will be bombed by Germany. It's called evacuation.

Uncle Don frowns all the time now and always seems angry.

He and Auntie Irene want to kill Hanno and send me away, don't they?

No one wants a German boy or a German dog now that they're at war with Germany. It's so unfair. It's not my fault Hitler wants to take over the world.

Lotte doesn't really understand either. All she can think about is turning seventeen next year.

"The minute I'm seventeen, the absolute *minute*," she

tells me, "I'll pack my bag, walk out of the Greens' house forever, and go and be a nurse. I've already got the forms and everything. I know exactly what to do."

She's said it so many times I'm fed up with hearing it.

When I start to moan at her on the street this morning about how I'm going to be sent away and I'll miss Hanno so much, she gets mad at me again.

"You're so selfish, Rudi!" she yells. "All you think about is yourself."

I start to cry, but she doesn't comfort me.

She just keeps on yelling. "Don't you care about Mutti and Papa and all the German Jews stuck with that monster Hitler and those crazy Nazis? If Britain doesn't win the war, they'll come over here and round up all the Jews. Don't you understand, you idiot? If the Nazis win, we Jews will never be safe!"

Her face goes very red and she's shaking. She doesn't give me a hug or anything when we say goodbye at the corner.

Lotte doesn't care about me anymore.

I'm just a pest, aren't I? I'm in everyone's way.

As I walk off to the hideout I think, *Hanno and I should run away and find a really good hiding place from the Nazis. They might land any day now.*

When we arrive in the clearing, Tilly and the other kids are standing around not saying anything, looking sad.

I think it's because of the war, but then Tilly says, "I'm sorry, everyone, but there's no one to look after the pets when we're evacuated. We're just going to have to set them free to fend for themselves."

Sidney catches my eye and I mutter, "*Nein*, no. Hanno won't go."

He shrugs and goes off to feed the tortoise.

We don't play Tarzan all day. I take Hanno for a walk in the woods and try to think of a plan for running away. I want to ask Sidney, but he spends all day at the top of his favorite tree with Miles. I even play my bugle a bit to cheer myself up, but it sounds hollow and strange under the big trees.

The sun starts to go down and I'm already late for tea, but I don't care. *The Evanses don't want Hanno and me, so they won't care if I miss tea. More food for them.*

It grows dark in the wood. I feel scared all by myself, so I sling my bugle around my back and call to Hanno, and we go back to the clearing.

Everyone is standing around Tilly, but this time they all seem really excited. People are patting each other on the back and grinning.

Miles hands Sidney some money.

"Rudi, mate," says Sidney when he catches sight of me. "Tilly's got a smashing plan to save the pets. We gotta go and ask a posh lady for help, but she lives miles away. We need some cash to pay my mate Len to take us in his truck. You got any money?"

I don't understand everything, but I have a silver shilling in my pocket that Lotte gave me last week. Maybe it could help save the pets and Hanno.

I pull out the shilling and hand it over.

"*Danke,* mate. Smashing!" Sidney says. "Come on, let's go."

∾

Once we've settled all the pets for the night, we set off. Everyone has a bike except me. I sit on Sidney's seat, my legs sticking out on each side, and he pedals us across the fields and over the canal. It's completely dark and there isn't a spot of light on the street.

"Don't bump into the lampposts and trees," warns Miles. "They have white lines painted around them."

I hadn't noticed before, but there are white lines on the curb too, so people won't have accidents in the blackout. *Very clever,* I think.

We stop at Sidney's place, and he goes to fetch Len. Soon we're bumping along the road in the back of the truck, which is open to the sky. We munch some apples that Tilly passed around.

It takes ages to get to the lady's gate, nearly half an

hour, someone says. When we jump down from the truck Tilly points the way through a big gate to a long, dark path.

"We have to go up that drive to the house," she says, and we all follow her.

I have a flashlight in my pocket and take it out.

"That's really useful, Rudi," Tilly says in a low voice.

Papa would be proud of me, I think. *Even if Lotte hates me now.*

The drive winds through a lot of trees. It feels quite creepy, and then we can see the outline of an enormous mansion, as wide as half our street. All the windows are blacked out for the war but there must be loads and loads.

These people are very rich, I think. *Maybe Tilly thinks they have enough space to look after all our pets.* Hanno doesn't take much space, and he only lived in an apartment back home in Germany.

The others don't seem as surprised as me when they see the house. Maybe lots of English people are rich enough to live like this. Sidney is leading the way; we follow him around the side and in through a small door. Then we have to stop because we hear men's voices. Sidney turns around and puts his finger to his lips but we're all too scared to make a sound. I'm holding my breath, and my knees are shaking.

The voices fade away. We go out of the room into a big square hall with doors on each side and a huge staircase coming down the middle. Tilly is trying to work out which door to open when we hear the men coming back.

"Quick, hide!" she says in a loud whisper.

Miles grabs my arm and pulls me behind the stairs, but the men spot Sidney. He runs off.

We all hold our breath. I'm so scared. Then we hear a door open and a lady's voice. After a minute the door closes.

Tilly looks around at us all and she whispers, "Everyone stay here. I'll go by myself. Sidney will be fine. He can take care of himself. If anything happens, make your getaway with Len. That way I'll be the only one to get into trouble. They'll never know you were here."

No one moves. All I can think is how completely brave she is, but I'm very worried about Sidney and even more worried about someone calling the police. If they find out I'm German, what will happen? Lotte will definitely never speak to me again.

Then Miles says, "Don't be silly, we're in this together."

The others all agree, and even I whisper, "*Ja!*"

Tilly gives a big sigh and shakes her head. Then she stands up and says, "Come on, then, better get it over with."

We all stand up too and move out from under the stairs. Tilly leads the way, marching over to the door and pushing it open.

My legs are shaking again as we go into a living room with two very posh-looking ladies sitting by a big fire.

Tilly starts to speak, but I can't really understand most of it. Then suddenly Sidney runs into the room, chased by the two men, and slithers across the floor. It's very funny, but I don't dare laugh. Tilly looked terrified. Miles sticks his hands in his pockets and turns red.

But one of the ladies—a very nice one with pointy eyebrows—sends the men away and asks Tilly to introduce us. She has a deep voice. She listens carefully to Tilly.

When Tilly says my name, she explains I'm German but not the enemy. I give my bow, and the lady gives me an approving look.

Then the lady says, "I work with an animal charity, and we're saving as many pets as we can. We completely disapprove of putting all these healthy animals down. And you children"— she looks around at all of us, nodding—"you seem to understand that we all have to pull together to defeat Mr. Hitler. I believe you children have the right qualities to help win this war."

Tilly nods, and the others look very serious. I nod too, so the lady will know I'm not a Nazi.

"I'll take all the pets," the lady goes on. "I'll send a truck at seven tomorrow morning. They will be looked after at my country home."

Tilly thanks her, and everyone grins.

The lady seems to understand that I'm a good German, not a Nazi. She's a bit like Sidney's mum, only with nicer clothes.

The best thing is that Hanno's going to be saved again—that's three times all together!

It's like a huge sandbag has suddenly slipped off my back.

We run down the dark drive and climb onto the truck. As we drive home I wonder what on earth I'm going to say to the Evanses about staying out so late and making everyone worried.

❦

Papa said to us the night before we left, "The British will be remembered forever for saving our Jewish children from Hitler. Don't make them sorry for taking you in."

As we arrive back at our streets I think, *If I run away, the Evanses will feel sorry they ever gave me a home. They might think Jews are not very nice people.*

I'm so tired I can't think anymore, and then I see Lotte running down the street. She's crying out in German, "Rudi, my darling little brother! You're safe! Oh, thank God! Thank God!"

She grabs me and almost squeezes me to death.

So I don't think she really hates me, does she?

12. Leaving Home Again

Tuesday, September 5, 1939

Carry a flashlight in the blackout.
Support the war effort.
Never forget you are Jewish—Lotte told me
*   that.*
Make a best friend. My best friend is Sidney.

I'm going to keep making notes even though Papa and Mutti are stuck in Germany for now. They'll really need them when they come over.

I'm on the bus going to be evacuated to the countryside. Tilly and her friends are sitting behind me. No one has any idea where we're going.

Sidney and Neville have already gone away with the whole school. But Mr. and Mrs. Evans wanted to make sure I had a nice family to go to. That's why I'm on Tilly's bus. Sidney's mum and Baby Tom will go later, once they're all settled somewhere. Sidney said he's worried their mum

won't find them, and I don't blame him. No one tells us anything, just like back home in Germany.

∾

Auntie Irene and Uncle Don hugged me even harder than
Lotte on Sunday night.

"We thought you'd run away, Rudi, lovey, because you
were frightened about the war starting," said Auntie Irene,
wiping her eyes on her apron.

"You don't need to be scared," said Uncle Don in his
kind voice. "You'll be safe in the countryside, and Auntie
Irene will come and visit you. That'll be fun, eh?"

I nodded. They really do care about me, and they honestly don't care that I'm a Jewish German boy. They've made
sure I have a nice family to be evacuated to away from the
bombing once it starts. I know now that they weren't the only
grown-ups to decide they must put their pets down. Alec
told me that thousands of people are doing the same thing all
over the country. It's utterly despicable, as Lotte says.

But in the end, I saved Hanno. That's all that matters.

Of course, they wanted to know why I was so late home.
I said I was playing outside and we all forgot the time. They
were so glad I was home, they didn't ask anything else.

Lotte thought I'd run away because she shouted at me.

As we walked back to the Evanses that night, she said,
"I'm so sorry I was angry with you, Rudi. I promise always to
take care of you. I'd be very lonely in England without you."

"Tilly said I was useful," I say.

"You *are*! Honestly! Very useful. I absolutely can't manage without you." She gave me another hug.

A lovely warm feeling went through me. We're all safe, including Hanno, and Lotte doesn't think I'm a pest.

"Do I really have to go away again?" I say.

"Yes, but I promise I will write you lots of letters and send you parcels and come and visit whenever I can," said Lotte.

Then she swung me around to face her. "Pioneers, right?"

"Pioneers," I said, and we grinned at each other.

~

We're out of London now and driving through the countryside. Tilly and her friends are whispering to each other behind me. At least I don't have to go on my own, but I don't really know my new family. Lotte says I have to be brave all over again.

I have Papa's bugle in my lap. I take out my bit of rag torn from his old shirt and polish the bugle until it shines and shines, even around the dented bit.

Then I take out my notebook and write:

Be cheerful.
Show you are a good German, not a Nazi.
Sidney says Tilly's a brick—a brick's a really
    good person—very strange.
Keep practicing the Hebrew prayers so you
    don't forget them.

Author's Note

This book was inspired by the little-known story of the destruction of pets at the outbreak of World War II in the United Kingdom. Some 750,000 pets were put down in the first few weeks of the war. People believed they could not feed their pets when rationing started and that the dogs would go mad in the bombing and bite people. The government announced that pets would not be allowed in the public shelters.

In doing my research, I read the story of two Jewish German children who had a place on a train to escape the Nazis but couldn't bring their dog with them. They couldn't bear to be parted from her, so they wrote to a British animal charity and asked the charity to take their dog and pay for quarantine. The charity agreed and the dog came to England.

My story about Rudi and his little dog, Hanno, was born.

Rudi and his sister, Lotte, came to England on special trains which became known as the Kindertransport. After Hitler came to power in Germany in 1933 life became very difficult and dangerous for German Jews. Then on the night of November 9, 1938, Nazi gangs attacked Jews all over Germany. They killed almost a hundred and injured many others. The gangs set fire to synagogues and smashed the glass in Jewish shops and homes. This terrible night became known as Kristallnacht—the Night of Broken Glass.

Kristallnacht was reported in newspapers all over the world. Jews in many countries became worried about the German Jews. British Jews, and many non-Jewish Britons also, asked the British government to help German Jews. The government said that it would allow Jewish children from Germany, Austria, and Czechoslovakia (which Hitler controlled) to come to Britain. When Britain declared war on Germany on September 3, 1939, the transports stopped.

You can find out more about the Kindertransport at the links below:

The Kindertransport Association
www.kindertransport.org/history.htm

The National Holocaust Centre and Museum
www.holocaust.org.uk/kindertransport

There are also two books for children about Kindertransport:

Drucker, Olga Levy. *Kindertransport* (New York: Henry Holt & Company), 1992.

Hodge, Deborah. *Rescuing the Children: The Story of the Kindertransport* (Toronto: Tundra), 2012.

Miriam Halahmy
London, England

Acknowledgments

I would like to thank the Harold Grinspoon Foundation and PJ Our Way for choosing this book for their wonderful program. Huge thanks to my publisher, Holiday House, and especially to my editor, Mary Cash, for her enthusiasm and her wise guidance in shaping this book. As always, deepest thanks to my agent, Anne Clark, who has given so much support to my writing.